FIRST DATES ARE FATAL

A SADIE MCINTYRE MYSTERY NOVELLA

BARBARA WALLACE

ALSO BY BARBARA WALLACE

The Suburbs Have Secrets

Backyards Have Bodies

To Peter, who puts up with a lot.

PROLOGUE

... "I'VE DECIDED it's time I look at living in something more permanent than a rental. You wouldn't happen to know a good real estate agent, would you? One who won't hesitate to throw herself at a killer if things get rough?"

"I might," I said with a smile. "Why don't you come by the office tomorrow and I'll show you some listings?"

"Can't tomorrow. My day's all tied up with, you know, crime things. How about we meet in about an hour? I could describe what I'm looking for and you can send me a list of suggestions?"

I looked at my watch. An hour would make it dinnertime. "Well, I was going to microwave some leftovers," I said, "but I could push my plans until later."

"Gilroy's has a dinner-for-two special. It's a Valentine's Day special, but there's no reason we can't take advantage of the deal, too, right?"

No reason besides some destroyed police evidence. On the other hand, I did have that new little black dress wasting away in my closet. And Gilroy's holiday specials were a great deal...

What the heck? It was only dinner, right? Dinner and, if I got lucky, another kiss. Only a fool would turn down that opportunity.

My mama didn't raise any fool. "I'll see you in an hour."

Happy Valentine's Day to me.

1

———

My palms were sweating like a sixteen-year-old's. Silly, since I wasn't going on a date—not a real one. Dan Bartlett wanted to buy a house; I sold real estate. Dinnertime was the most convenient time to meet.

Okay, so it was Valentine's Day night, and the last time Dan Bartlett and I saw each other, he kissed me—an act that moved our relationship bad idea territory and into simmering possibility land. That was no reason for me to freak out. And if I happened to squeeze myself into shapewear and a new black dress... Nothing wrong with wanting to look nice. I always dressed well for clients. Even the ones without broad shoulders and silky-rough voices.

We agreed to meet at Gilroy's Tavern at seven p.m. I arrived at 6:50. Never let it be said I wasn't punctual. Besides, I knew from experience that I'd need extra time to find a parking space. As it was, I ended up parking behind the dry cleaners across the street.

I kicked myself as soon as I stepped out of the car and the wind blew up my skirt. New England was in the grips of a polar vortex with nighttime temperatures in the single digits and a stinging north wind. The smart people wore their heavy winter coats.

Even Bartlett had exchanged his customary leather jacket for a gray overcoat. He met me at the crosswalk, and I saw that beneath his wool coat he wore a soft green sweater. He'd shaved, too, not that it meant any more than my little black dress.

"I expected there'd be a crowd because of Valentine's Day, but this looks like everyone in Woodbridge is here," he said. "Is the brisket that good?"

Every Valentine's Day, and only on Valentine's Day, Gilroy's Tavern offered its famous two-for-one brisket special. Slow roasted for hours and smothered in Gilroy's secret maple cream sauce, it melted in your mouth.

"Better than good. Try otherworldly," I said. "Divorced couples who hate each other have reunited for the night rather than give up their reservation and miss out. Come to think of it, how did you manage to get a table on short notice?"

He flashed what I'd come to call his Bartlett smirk, an annoyingly indulgent smile that charmed without giving away a thing. "Let's just say I have my connections."

"One of those connections wouldn't be named Rob Carmichael, would it?" My best friend was the most popular man in Woodbridge. Also, the most handsome which no doubt contributed to his popularity.

"I take the fifth," Bartlett replied. No matter. His non-reply said everything, as did the pale pink tinting his cheek-bones. I looked away to hide my smile.

Once upon a time, Gilroy's Tavern hosted Sons of Liberty meetings. Some in town would say it hasn't been renovated since then, but that's an exaggeration. The pewter and décor were solid mid-seventies, not that the dated interior affected the restaurant's popularity. Bartlett and I stepped inside to discover a line waiting to check in. We weren't surprised, then, when the hostess told us they were running behind schedule and asked for our patience. The poor woman looked like she might wilt with relief when Bartlett accepted the delay with a smile. I could only imagine the craziness being thrown in her direction. Hunger pains could turn normally mild people into jerks. And turn jerks into bigger jerks.

Case in point, the barrel-chested man in a fisherman's sweater who took my place at the hostess stand. Ben Cartwright, real estate developer extraordinaire and self-appointed King of Woodbridge.

I tried to step into the lounge and give him space, but there wasn't any space to give. I ended up tucked behind the spindles, trying not to eavesdrop. Unfortunately, the proximity—and Ben's booming voice—made ignoring them impossible.

"I'm sorry, Mr. Cartwright," the hostess replied. "Our larger parties are taking longer than expected. If you'd like to have a drink in the lounge, I'll come—"

"I didn't come here for a drink. I want to eat. Why bother making a reservation if you're not gonna honor them?"

"I realize it's frustrating, but this is our busiest day of the year."

"I don't care how busy it is. You don't make people wait when they have a reservation. Now find us a table, or do I have to talk to your boss about your crappy service?"

The woman's chin wobbled, but she kept her composure throughout Ben's tantrum. "I'll check the dining room."

"You do that," Ben snapped.

Bartlett appeared at my shoulder. While I'd been watching Ben, Dan had gone to the bar for drinks.

Cabernet for me, diet cola for him. "I see Ben's being his charming self," he remarked.

"Even more than usual," I replied.

Back in the 90s, when the suburban exodus started expanding west, Ben Cartwright bet on Woodbridge being the next desirable location. Leveraging himself to his eyeballs, he bought up as many of the local farms as he could and turned the land into housing lots. The bet paid off. Woodbridge doubled in population, and Ben became a multi-millionaire. Along with his wealth came the assumption that he had priority over everyone else. He was just like my father, Joey Albano, only Ben never killed a man for crossing him. So far as I knew, anyway.

"Mr. Cartwright—"

It wasn't the hostess returning, but a well-dressed man with a pompadour. "I'm very sorry for the wait. They're cleaning your table now. Why don't I have the server bring you a bottle of wine on the house?"

"Try two bottles," Ben replied. "The best cabernet you've got, not the cheap house brand you pawn off on everybody else."

I looked at my glass. My wine didn't taste so bad.

Having terrified the hostess to his satisfaction, Ben shouldered back to the pub table where his family stood. I recognized Ben's second wife, Bethany, as well as his grown daughters Kim and Tracy, and Kim's husband Steve Cho.

"The manager's giving us a couple of bottles of wine," he said, loud enough for the entire bar to hear. I wondered if Ben even knew how to speak softly. "I'm telling ya, customer service's gone to hell in this country."

"I don't know why you insisted on coming here in the first place. The service is always terrible. If we'd gone to Entrecote like I suggested, we'd be on dessert by now."

"Give it a rest, Bethany," Ben snapped. "I already told

you I didn't want to go to Entrecote, I wanted Gilroy's brisket."

"That's another thing. All that grease and heavy cream sauce." Bethany was one of those uber-fit people with zero percent body fat. Woodbridge seemed to attract them. "I can hear your arteries clogging already."

"I said give it a rest."

"You could have always stayed home if you hate Gilroy's so much," Tracy Cartwright said.

"You know perfectly well I'm not skipping your father's birthday dinner. I even ordered a special cake. Lemon with raspberry filling."

"With thirty candles to mark the age difference?"

"Give Bethany a break, Tracy." Steve Cho rode to Bethany's defense. "She's trying to make the night special."

Bethany flashed him a smile before turning back to Ben. "I'm sorry I'm being cranky, sweetheart. We're a little hangry is all. Feel the little guy swishing around? He's hungry."

Ben pressed his beefy hand to her abdomen. Whatever he felt made him grin like a kid. "That's my boy! A Cartwright through and through."

Tucked in our corner, Bartlett and I listened to the conversation along with the rest of the lounge. "They certainly dominate a room, don't they?" Bartlett remarked.

"Woodbridge's own traveling reality show," I said. "Why watch Real Housewives when you've got the Cartwrights?" Whenever the family showed up, you could count on a show. They liked drawing attention to themselves, I decided. Why else would they insist on talking loud enough for the whole world to know their business?

The front door opened, and in came a gush of cold air accompanied by a woman wearing a black puffer coat, Woodbridge's coat *de rigueur* for winter. Half the people in town wore one, including me, our socioeconomic status advertised by the location of the outer label. Embroidered logos on the right shoulder for regular folk, a red Arctic patch on the arm for people like Ben.

The woman who entered had a shoulder logo. I recognized her immediately as Ben's former assistant. Delfina something-or-other. Every so often, he'd send her over to the office with paperwork.

She spotted Ben's party and made a beeline for the group. A woman with a mission. Faster than you could say hello, Ben jumped to his feet and intercepted her. The pair moved to a corner to speak. Back at the table, Bethany looked ready to toss her water glass.

Over in the corner, Ben was glowering. The conversation ended and Delfina thrust a crumpled envelope into his hand before hurrying away. Ben stared at the envelope for a few beats, then stuffed it in his back pocket.

Upon his return, Bethany wasted no time voicing her displeasure. "What was she doing here?"

Instead of answering, Ben waved his empty tumbler in the air. "Hey! I need a Scotch over here."

On the other side of the room, the bartenders exchanged a look, one that, had it been my order, would have me worried someone spit in my glass.

Meanwhile, Bethany refused to be ignored. "Did you hear me, Ben? What did she want?"

"Nothing," he replied. "Wanted to wish me a happy birthday, is all."

"And beg for her old job back, no doubt," Steve said. "Two months since we let her go, and she's still trying to get back in your good graces. You'd think the woman would get the hint."

"Because she's crazy," Bethany said. "Always hanging around, showing up where we are. The person who kept calling you and hanging up the other night? I bet it was her, stalking you."

"I've already told you those were spam calls. No one's stalking anybody. The woman simply wanted to say happy birthday."

"I don't know, Ben, Bethany might have a point. Delfina does always seem to be around. I swear I saw her parked by your house yesterday," Steve said.

Kim, who had been more interested in her white wine than the conversation, looked up. She was always the quietest of the bunch. "You were at Dad's house yesterday?"

Her question was ignored as Bethany continued ranting. "I don't know why you don't get a restraining order. I've told you a million times the woman freaks me out. Gotten so I'm afraid to be alone in the house. I mean, who knows what she could do?"

"And I told you, I'll handle Delfina. There's no need to drag the police into it."

"Bethany's got a point," Steve said. "I think going to the police might not be a bad idea."

"That what you think, Steve?" Ben's question was more like a challenge. He leaned back, arms folded across his broad chest.

"What I think…" Without breaking eye contact, Steve mimicked Ben's pose. "Is that if going to the police makes your wife feel safer—"

Kim cut her husband off. "Why don't you let Daddy worry about Bethany's feelings," she said.

"You should listen to your wife," Ben said. "I'll handle Delfina."

"But—"

"I said I'll handle it, Bethany!" he snapped. The rest of the family flinched as if they'd heard a gunshot. "End of discussion. Where the hell is the Scotch I asked for? And where's that hostess? We should be halfway through dinner by now."

I turned to Bartlett who was struggling not to smile He shook his head "Well. That was—"

"Entertaining?" I suggested.

"Interesting," he replied. "Are you sure they aren't filming an actual reality show?"

I shook my head. "Just your everyday, ordinary Cartwright family dysfunction," I replied.

And we had yet to sit down for dinner. Who knew what drama might show up with the brisket?

2

———

"What kind of house are you looking for?" I asked once we were seated. At a table next to the Cartwright party, I might add, much to Bartlett's amusement.

He shrugged and reached for the butter. Twenty minutes of smelling maple and fresh bread had us starving. As soon as the frazzled waitress set down a basket of rolls, we pounced. "Anything really, so long as it has four walls. I'm not picky."

"Keith Koenig told me the same thing. Two years later we're still trying to find the perfect house." I almost had him sold on the last property, but then Alex Fitzgerald turned up dead in the backyard and scared him off. "Which reminds me, where do you stand on dead bodies?"

He looked up. "In general, or as a house feature?"

"House feature. I don't know if you've noticed but recently some of the properties on the market were—"

"Murder scenes?"

"I was going to say murder *adjacent*. Only two were actual murder scenes."

"Correction noted." The waitress returned, and we

paused our conversation long enough to confirm that, like everyone else, we'd have the brisket. "To answer your question," he continued, once she had gone, "I'm willing to overlook a dead body if the property has a decent-sized kitchen."

"That's very pragmatic of you," I noted, although hardly surprising. Bartlett was no-nonsense through and through. He saved his energy for what mattered. Like the facts and the truth. An image of burning evidence flashed through my mind. I reached for my wine to wash it away.

"You are greedy, selfish, slimy…" A middle-aged woman wearing a puffy coat and boots stomped into the dining room and headed straight for—where else?—the Cartwrights.

"That's the ex-wife," I whispered to Bartlett's arched brow.

Her face red with anger, Patty Cartwright thrust a crumpled paper at Ben Cartwright's chest. "You're lucky I don't kill you right here. Who do you think you are?"

Ben focused on the roll he was buttering. "Why don't you screech a little louder, Patty, there might be some people in the lounge who didn't hear you."

"Oh, I'm sorry, am I making a scene?" She raised her voice. "Am *I embarrassing you*? Tough crap. Being embarrassed is the least you deserve. Do the girls know what you're doing?"

"Know what?" Kim asked. "What did you do, Dad?"

Ben opened his mouth, but Patty answered before he could get the words out. "Your father wants to cut off my alimony."

"What?" Tracy and Kim cried in unison.

"He's petitioned the court to stop making payments."

"You can't do that," Tracy replied. Kim simply stared at him with a shell-shocked expression.

"Why not? Your mother is making plenty of money on her own these days. There's no need for her to bleed me dry on top of it."

"Bleed you dry? You wouldn't have a thing if it weren't for me. You owe me that money, Ben Cartwright."

"*You owe me, Ben Cartwright*," Ben mocked. "You got a house, a Mercedes, and four years of my money. My days of paying you are over."

"Trust me, you haven't begun to pay. Don't touch me, you creep." The last part was directed to the manager who was attempting to steer Patty out of the restaurant. She wrenched free of his grip. Bartlett set his napkin on the table, preparing to step in if the situation escalated.

"Mom, please. Don't let him push your buttons. You're better than this," Kim urged.

"Let your lawyer handle things," Tracy added.

"You should listen to your daughters," Ben said. "Before you make a bigger fool out of yourself."

Patty glowered at him. I crossed my fingers that she would back down. Drama was one thing, violence was another. Slowly, her shoulders sagged. "I'm going. For Kim and Tracy's sake," she added. "But this isn't over. Marriage is till death do us part, buddy, and that includes alimony."

———

"One thing about Woodbridge, it's never short on drama," I said to Bartlett. We were one of the last pairs to leave the restaurant. The Cartwrights left before dessert; Patty's outburst illed what little good mood they had. "Maybe there's something in the water supply."

"Maybe. You are all a little crazy. Although," he said, turning to look at me, "I'm discovering I like crazy. Some, anyway."

I blushed. Leave it to Dan Bartlett to turn crazy into a compliment.

"Ben knows how to push Patty's buttons, that's for sure," I said. "I'm glad her daughters convinced her to walk away. Still, the way Ben's treated her over the years… No one would blame her for taking a swing."

"Fortunately, calmer heads prevailed. I didn't relish making an arrest before dessert."

We reached my car. Reaching my car meant saying goodnight, and saying goodnight meant… what? How did things work in the modern dating world? He'd paid for dinner. What did that mean? Bartlett didn't strike me as the hooking-up-in-the-backseat kind of guy, which is what it meant when I was a kid. Did I ask him to follow me back to my place? To do what? Did I want him to follow me back?

There had to be a thousand butterflies in my stomach waiting for me to make up my mind. It was up to instinct, I decided. Whatever popped out of my mouth. I took a deep breath.

"I've got an early shift in the morning," he said before any words came out.

"Oh." The butterflies fell in a lump. So much for worrying about next moves. "Right," I said. "I need to get up early myself. This was fun."

I searched through my bag pretending to look for my keys. "I'll, um, pull together a list of potential properties for you and send them over."

"There's no rush." His gloved hand caught mine, stopping my faux rummaging. Beneath the layers of cool leather, my skin grew warm. I looked up to discover him looking at my mouth. "Would it be all right if I kissed you goodnight?"

All right? The butterflies were cheering it was so all right. "Very," I whispered.

"Good." His kiss was slow and deliberate. The kind of kiss that made your knees buckle and your lungs forget how to breathe. When we broke away, my back was pressed against the car, and my arms were around his neck. I didn't remember moving.

Taking the keys from my bag, Bartlett unlocked my door. "Good night, Sadie."

I think I said goodnight back. The ghost of the kiss lasted the entire drive home. I could still feel it when the phone rang and woke me early the next morning.

With my eyes closed, I put the phone to my ear, dreaming of being greeted by a gravelly whisper. Instead, an excited British accent sounded in my ear. "You're not going to believe what I heard," Rob Carmichael said.

I looked at the time. 5:45 a.m. "Rob, I love you, but do you have any idea what time it is?" The sun wouldn't be up for another hour, for God's sake. "Couldn't whatever it is wait until we get coffee?"

"Someone shot Ben Cartwright."

Suddenly, I was wide awake.

3

———

An hour later, I walked into Cuppa Joe's Coffee Shop, the aroma of fresh coffee and blueberry muffins reminding me why it was the most popular coffee house in town.

Rob waved to me from his usual table, his pretty face, and by pretty, I mean extraordinarily handsome, a welcome sight. Until that morning, he'd been in seclusion, hiding from prying eyes.

"Took you long enough." He pushed a paper cup in my direction, wincing slightly as he did so. Peeking out from the neckline of his cashmere sweater, I could see part of the bandage covering a gash on his shoulder, left there when a killer had slashed him with a pair of scissors.

Knowing he didn't want to talk about the injury, I pretended not to notice and sat down. "Give me a break. I was in bed when you called. Not everyone can bound out of bed Instagram-ready. Some of us need to do our hair and makeup. Now what's this about Ben Cartwright being murdered?"

"Last night sometime. They found his body in the park early this morning. Shot in the back."

And he knew this how? I frowned. "You're not running in the middle of the night again, are you?"

"No, I'm not running in the middle of the night. I learned my lesson the last time."

"Good." It was a weird habit, one that got him accused of murder. If it weren't for a yappy dog and doorbell cameras, he might be sitting in jail awaiting trial.

"Police scanner app. Picks up police radios from all over the country. After all the crazy stuff that's happened in town, I'm surprised you haven't downloaded the app yourself. Don't you want to know what Tim is getting up to?"

"Tim would kill me if he caught me listening to the police scanner." I was hiding enough secrets from my son as it was. Big ones. Like our entire family history. I didn't need to add petty annoyances to the pile.

"Good thing Uncle Rob is doing it for you then, isn't it?" Rob replied with a grin. "Anyway, I was scrambling eggs when I heard the dispatcher report a 10-17 in Tunnell Park. That means possible gunshot, in case you didn't know."

I knew.

"Anyway, a little while later, an officer came on to say they'd found a body and that it was Ben Cartwright. Or to be more precise, she said 'Holy Bleep, it's Ben Cartwright'."

I echoed the officer's response as I sank into a nearby chair. I wasn't friends with Ben—I'm not sure anyone was truly friends with the man—but it was still a shock. "Dan and I saw him just last night at Gilroy's."

Rob arched an eyebrow. "Dan now, is it?"

"It was Ben's birthday," I continued. "The whole clan was there making a scene, as usual. Even Patty." I told him what happened in the dining room. "*Bartlett* was afraid he'd have to intervene."

"Cutting off her alimony because she's surviving without him. Sounds like Ben. Wouldn't blame Patty if she popped him one," he added over the rim of his cup.

"No one would." I hope she didn't though. I liked Patty, the few times I'd dealt with her, back when she helped run the company. After Ben hit it big, she'd remained the same down-to-earth suburban mom she'd always been. Too down to earth in Ben's eyes since he dumped her for a younger, more sophisticated model. "He's not worth ruining her life over. Did you say they found him in Tunnell Park?"

"Yep. Near the swing set."

"Weird. Wonder what he was doing there?"

"Taking a walk, maybe? Not everyone goes to bed at ten."

"In February? In the middle of the night? What time did you hear the call?"

"Two. Two-thirty," he replied.

"Several hours after he left the restaurant, then. Wait a second." The rest of his comment sunk in. "Why were you scrambling eggs at two in the morning?"

Rob gave a kind of boyish shrug as a blush spread along his perfect cheekbones. A look, I imagine, killed the young girls in his boyband days, and for that matter, the students in his British Lit class. "Might have had some company," he murmured.

And here I thought he was hiding out to avoid gossip. I leaned across the table. "Anyone I know?" There was that attentive EMT the night he was injured. Certainly would explain his suddenly downloading the scanner app.

He narrowed his eyes. "Did I ask for details about your Valentine's date?"

"You had a Valentine's date?"

I looked up to see my son, Tim standing there wearing his police uniform. "Hi, honey. I didn't see you walk in," I said. "Rob just told me someone shot Ben Cartwright."

He looked back and forth between us. "How…?"

"Scanner app," Rob and I said simultaneously.

"Is it true? Or did the officer make a mistake?"

"You know I can't say anything until the news is made public."

"That's a yes then."

"No comment. Did you seriously have a date last night?"

"I had dinner with a friend, and you needn't sound so surprised." Seriously, he made it sound like I was living in a cloister.

"Mom, you haven't gone on a date since the last administration."

"That is s not true. I go out plenty."

"I don't count," Rob said.

Normally I'd remind Rob that he wasn't exactly racking up dating points himself, but his Valentine's sleepover put him up on points meaning I had to settle for muttering, "I didn't realize you two were so invested in my romantic life."

"I just want you to be happy," Tim said. "Dad's gone, and someday I'll have a family of my own. I don't want to see you old and living alone with seventeen cats."

"If I have seventeen cats, then I won't be living alone, will I?"

"You know what I mean, Ma."

I did, and while I wouldn't say so out loud, I appreciated the sentiment. Though dollars to doughnuts, he'd change his mind if he knew my date had been with Dan Bartlett. No one wants their mother in a relationship with their boss. Not that Dan and I were in one. A couple of kisses, dinner, and an erotic dream did not a relationship make.

"Don't you have a crime scene to protect?" I asked, changing the subject.

"Nope, not this time. Bartlett wants to canvas the neighborhood to see if anyone heard or saw anything unusual. I'm here on break to grab a coffee, then it's off to knock on doors."

You could hear the excitement in his voice. I couldn't blame the kid. Canvassing for witnesses meant they were starting to trust his skills.

When I was eight months pregnant, I had a massive panic attack. What did I know about raising a family? I'd torpedoed mine. Sent my father and fiancé up the river. My mother wished me dead. And here I was about to become responsible for a baby?

My late husband, Jim, took my face in his hands and made me take a deep breath. "We're going to be all right," he'd said. "You and me, we can do it."

Now here he was, our baby boy, all grown up. I watched with pride as Tim stepped to the back of the coffee line. Jim had been right. But then, he usually was.

"Oh hey, I almost forgot," Tim called over. "Detective Bartlett had a message he wanted passed along if I ran into you."

"He did?" My insides gave a little skip, even though I knew there was no reason to be excited. We were talking about a message delivered via my son, after all.

"He told me to tell you that there was no need to deliver the Widow Cartwright a casserole."

"Sounds like someone's on to your trick," Rob said. Delivering food to the victim's family had been my go-to for gaining access in the last two murders. Nothing says

"I'm sorry for your loss, and may I ask a few questions" like a meatloaf or chicken pot pie.

"Tell Detective Bartlett that contrary to what he might think, I don't show up with a casserole every time someone dies. Only the deaths where I have a personal stake. I have no intention of getting involved in this investigation. Seriously," I added at Rob's and Tim's skeptical expressions. "My amateur sleuth days are over. Dan Bartlett's going to have to solve this one on his own."

4

———————

A short while later, I left Cuppa and drove to Putnam Law Associates to attend a closing. No sooner had I parked my car than my phone dinged.

DB: On my own, huh?

I smiled at my screen. Bartlett didn't waste words.

SM: You talked to Tim.

DB: So did you.

SM: I can't believe you warned me off through my son.

DB: Better safe than sorry. You DO have a habit of getting involved in my investigations.

SM: Not this one.

Dots appeared next to his caller ID, then disappeared as he deleted his response and wrote a new one.

DB: Are you sure?

Was he kidding? Did he honestly think I would poke my nose into his murder investigation? So yeah, I got involved the last time, but that was to help Rob. And the time before, I was a potential suspect. With Ben, there was no personal connection. Other than seeing him a few hours before he died, that is.

SM: I can't believe you think I would run over to Bethany Cartwright's with a chicken pot pie to pump her for information about her husband.

DB: You must admit, there is an established pattern.

SM: I'll have you know bringing food to families when there's a crisis is a time-honored tradition.

DB: You should be flattered, you know.

SM: I should? Why?

He had Tim tell me to mind my own business. What was flattering about being called nosy?

DB: Because I was standing at a murder scene thinking about you.

Oh. When he put it that way... The idea of Dan Bartlett thinking about me while combing the playground was strangely flattering.

Speaking of…

> SM: Do you know why Ben was in the park in the middle of the night?

> DB: I've got a few theories.

> SM: Like what?

> DB: Thought you weren't getting involved?

Damn. Busted with my own argument.

———

THE CLOSING WAS ROUTINE. A young couple with a new baby, they reminded me of when Jim and I bought our first house, minus the assumed identity. I passed over the keys with sincere wishes for the future.

Tracy and Patty Cartwright were getting out of their car as I exited the building. Seeing them caught me by surprise. I expected them to be home dealing with Ben's death.

I went over to offer my condolences. Patty looked terrible, like she didn't sleep. Her black puffer coat brought out her pale skin along with the circles under her eyes.

Tracy's eyes on the other hand, were bright and sharp. Her cheeks and lips had color, too.

They acknowledged me with cheerless smiles. I told them that Woodbridge wouldn't be the same without Ben's presence. "How is everyone doing?"

"Coping, for the most part," Patty replied with a shrug. "Poor Kimmy's a wreck. Other than Bethany, she took the news the hardest. Finally had to give her one of my Xanax, so she'd settle down."

"It's a shock. To think I saw him just last night celebrating his birthday at Gilroy's."

The color—what little there was—drained from Patty's face. "I take it that means you saw the fight I had with Ben. Not my finest moment, that."

"Happens. We've all lost our temper at the wrong time," I said.

"It's just… He always knows—I mean knew—how to push my buttons. I thought I'd stopped letting him get under my skin, but that stunt with the alimony…" She shrugged again. "Like I said to that detective, it's a moot point now."

"Do they have any idea who could have shot him?"

"Anyone who lives in Eastern Massachusetts."

"Tracy—"

"What? It's the truth, isn't it? Dad was a bully. No sense in pretending otherwise. Only a matter of time before karma caught up with him."

Clearly, Tracy wasn't taking her father's murder as hard as her sister.

"Dad liked to pretend he was this big-time maverick businessman. Go big or go home. That sort of thing," she said. "He used to have this big motivation poster in his office when I was a kid that said, 'You can't stop the steamroller,' remember Mom?"

"I remember. Once your father got something in his head, he wouldn't stop until he got what he wanted," Patty replied.

Like Bethany?

"And to hell with who he hurt in the process," Tracy said bitterly.

Interesting, I thought. Patty kicked Ben out after she discovered his affair with Bethany. At the time, people in town assumed it was a typical case of a rich man tossing over the dowdy wife for a younger model, especially since the ink on the divorce papers was barely dry when he and Bethany flew to Vegas. But now it sounded like pursuing and conquering was a pattern. Could that be why Ben was in the park? Had he been meeting his latest conquest?

"I better get inside," Patty said. "Glen bills by the hour. Don't want to pay for extra minutes if I don't have to. He's annoyed enough at my asking for a refund that he'd probably bill double."

Patty wasn't wrong. Glen could be a petty bastard. Several years ago, I turned down a second date with him, and I swear he's nitpicked my closing documents ever since. "You coming?" she asked Tracy.

Her daughter shook her head. "You go ahead. I need a cigarette. I'll meet you at Stillman's." Stillman's Funeral Home was a block down the street.

"Your mom's helping you plan the funeral?" I was surprised. Shouldn't that role fall to the widow and not the ex-wife?

"She didn't want me going alone," Tracey replied as she rifled through her oversized bag. Watching her, I was suddenly struck by how much she resembled her father. Same square jaw and stern set of her mouth. Same aggressive manner. Wouldn't take no for an answer. I heard she worked as a sales rep for one of the Boston pharmaceutical companies. A top performer, I bet.

"Nice of your mother to help," I said. "Planning a funeral alone can be a tough job."

"I'm not sure what kindness has to do with it. More like she's afraid I'll tell the funeral director to dump Dad's ashes out back. Surprised?"

"A little," I admitted.

"You shouldn't be. I wasn't joking when I said my dad was a jerk. Aha, found them."

She waved the gold and white pack triumphantly. A moment later a trail of smoke curled in the crisp winter air. "You were there last night; heard the garbage he was pulling with Mom's alimony. He always treated her like dirt. Making her do everything, then taking all the credit. God, I needed this." Her eyes fluttered shut as she pulled the smoke into her lungs. When she spoke again, it billowed like clouds from her nose and mouth. "You know Mom's the whole reason his company was a success, right?"

I'd heard the story. How, after Ben irritated the farmers with his hard-sell tactics, Patty had come in and smoothed things out. Her calm, lowkey approach convinced several of the farmers to reconsider Ben's offer. And, because of her business background, she took care of the company finances. If it weren't for her careful managing of the books, Cartwright Real Estate Development wouldn't have turned such a large profit.

"There wouldn't be a Cartwright Real Estate if it wasn't for her, and what does Dad do? He cheats her out of her share of the business and then tries to cut off her alimony. And now here she is stepping up to help plan his funeral because my sister and his 'wife' can't deal. He didn't deserve her. Or any of us, really. Except Bethany."

She flicked her ashes to the ground, then ground them with the toe of her boot as though doubling down on the disgust. She was giving off some serious hate vibes.

And yet, she associated with him. Last night's birthday dinner wasn't the first time I'd see the entire family together. Their traveling dysfunction show was known all over town. Why spend so much time with the man?

"The only reason any of us hung with him was the money," she said, reading my mind. "He made it very clear if we ever wanted to see a penny, we had to play the happy family whenever he wanted. No way I was going to let that fake blond reap the benefits of Mom's hard work. Bad enough she went and got herself pregnant. Talk about perfect timing."

"What do you mean? Are you saying she and your father weren't getting along?"

"Let's just say things between her and Dad were getting frosty," Tracy said. "Dad didn't like how much money she was spending updating the house."

She went on to tell me how, a few weeks earlier, Tracy had arrived early for one of her father's required dinners and walked in on them fighting over bathroom renovations Bethany wanted.

"Seven grand for a freaking tub?" Ben had screamed. "And a fireplace? For what? So we can toast marshmallows while we take a dump?"

"Sounds like some bathroom," I remarked.

"Bethany said a designer of her 'stature'" —Tracy framed the word in air quotes— "needed her house to reflect a certain level of elegance. Which made Dad totally flip. 'Your company hasn't made a dime in years', he said. 'All your fancy client dinners and trade shows and not a thing to show for it but a bunch of bills.' Called her spending out of control, and he was putting her on a budget. No more traveling to shows. No more fancy bath-tubs. You can imagine how well that went over."

"Poorly?"

"Thermonuclear poor. Dad said if Bethany didn't like it, she could get out. Then the stick turned blue, and Dad changed his tune. Getting pregnant with Dad's son was the best thing that could have happened to her," Tracy said as she flicked the cigarette with her thumb. "Well, second best if you count last night."

Implication hung in the air, like the cigarette smoke, thick and obvious. "You're not suggesting Bethany…?"

"I'm not suggesting anything," she replied. "I'm simply noting that she's had two fortuitous coincidences this year. Now if you'll excuse me, I've got a funeral to plan."

She tossed her cigarette into a drift and walked away. I pulled out my phone and called Bartlett.

5

———

"WHAT THE HELL kind of town builds a public park and then doesn't install security cameras?"

Bartlett stood with his hands on his hips looking like he expected an answer. I arched my brow. "Hello to you, too."

"Sorry. It's been a frustrating morning," he said as he took a seat across from me. The sharpness receded, replaced by a slow smile, not unlike the one that followed our kiss. "Hello," he said.

"Hello," I said returning the smile.

We were at the Golden Panda, a cheap Chinese restaurant at the strip mall. Strictly a deep-fried and heavy sweet sauce kind of place, it was a favorite in town when you wanted a fast, bad-for-you-but-oh-so-good meal. It was also a local cop favorite. Bartlett and I had eaten there before, when we were we were working to clear Rob's name.

The restaurant, all six laminated booths of it, was sparsely decorated: a pair of illuminated pictures of the Imperial palace and a Good Fortune Cat on the counter. That day red and gold banners were strung along the walls, leftovers from Lunar New Year. They gave the place a festive feel.

"I hope you don't mind, but I figured you'd be on a tight schedule, so I went ahead and ordered you a number three special," I said. Sweet and sour chicken, pork fried rice, and an egg roll. Same order he had the last time. "And to answer your question, the town council put the project out for bid, but the numbers came back too high. That's why we only have them in the parking lot." Ben, from what I gathered, was found on the older playground, on the east side of the pond. The parking lights didn't reach there. The perfect location for a clandestine meeting.

"Did you learn anything from the parking lot cameras?" I asked although I'd already guessed the answer.

"Only that Woodbridge rolls up the sidewalks after midnight. Not a single car entered the lot last night. Same for the office lot on the other side of the road."

"And no one who lives on the street saw anything? What about the person who called about the gunshots?" Even as I asked, I knew the answer. If Tim's canvassing had turned up evidence, Bartlett wouldn't be so annoyed at the security cameras.

"Late enough that everyone was asleep. The gunshots woke them. We did find Cartwright's car. About a quarter mile from the park."

Only one reason why a man would park a block away from two empty parking lots and then go stand in the darkest section of the park. "Sounds like Ben didn't want anyone to know he was there."

"So, it would seem. He was meeting someone; we know that much. There was a note on the front seat. You didn't see this from me." He pulled up a picture on his cellphone and slid it toward me. I saw a crumpled birthday card lying on the seat of what I assumed was Ben Cartwright's car.

"From whom?"

He shook his head. "No name. Just the words 'Tunnell Park' and a time. 1:30 a.m."

I took a longer look. *Happy Birthday to a Special Someone* stared back at me, the fanciful lettering mocking in its cheeriness. "So, the killer lured Ben to the park?"

"Or someone else did and saw the murder. Either way, I'm very interested in talking to them."

The server called out our number and we put our conversation on hold while we focused on our food. Or rather, Bartlett focused on his food, I focused on getting my chopsticks to work properly. No matter how many times I tried to master them, I ended up spilling more than reached my mouth. On my third try to scoop up rice, only to have the grains flutter back to the plate, I heard Bartlett's low chuckle.

"Didn't your mother teach you that you shouldn't laugh at the inept?" I said.

"You're not inept. You're just doing it wrong."

Same thing, wasn't it? Before I could ask, he reached across the table for my hand. "You're trying to move both chopsticks, which doesn't work. You want to hold the bottom stick still while controlling the top one with your fingers."

Gently, he took the chopsticks from my hand. "The trick," he said, "is to hold the bottom stick like you were holding a pen," he said, letting it rest between my thumb and forefinger. I thought of telling him that Rob had already given me this lesson—several times—but then he'd take his hand away and I was enjoying his touch.

"You want to choke up too," he continued. "Like a baseball bat. The lower your grip and the less stick you have, the easier it is to control. Then, you grip the top stick with your thumb and your first two fingers. Try it."

I did as I was told and pinched a piece of chicken. And, just like when Rob tried to teach me, watched it fall back to my plate with a plop. Sauce splattered the table. A second and third try yielded the same results.

Bartlett, God love him, tried to hide his smirk. "Maybe you should get that fork after all," he said.

I did, and for the next few minutes happily shoveled rice into my mouth with abandon. I was on my last forkful when Bartlett asked about my text. Distracted by deep-fried goodness and chopstick lessons, I'd completely forgotten the reason I asked him to meet. I told him about Ben and Bethany's marital issues."

"Frosty, you say?" Reaching across the table, he pinched a piece of broccoli and popped it into his mouth. "You know this because…?"

"Tracy Cartwright told me. And before you start in about getting involved, I didn't seek her out. I ran into her and Patty as I was coming out of my closing."

"And naturally you decided to talk to them."

"I stopped to offer my condolences. Would you rather I'd ignored them? Don't answer that," I added before he could open his mouth.

"According to Tracy, Ben and Bethany had been fighting a lot. Ben wasn't happy about all the money Bethany was spending on the house and put her on a tight budget. He also reined in her business expenses. No more traveling or fancy dinners. Apparently, the design firm was losing money."

Bartlett chewed on a second piece of broccoli while he digested what I'd told him. "Interesting," he said, finally.

"I thought you might think that." I sat back, pleased with myself. Here I was not getting involved in the case and still bringing Bartlett useful information. Not going to lie. His acknowledgment made me feel good. "But that doesn't explain why Ben was at the park last night. Unless…" A thought hit me. "It had something to do with Bethany."

It certainly would explain Ben's clandestine behavior. He wouldn't want word of his late-night activities getting back to her.

"Perhaps," Bartlett replied, although his furrowed expression suggested he had another theory. "Tracy said they were arguing about money?"

"She bought a seven thousand dollar bathtub," I replied.

"You're kidding. Why?"

Said the man whose only requirements were four walls and a roof. "You'd be surprised what people spend money on during a makeover. Renee once sold a house where the owner installed a coffee station and television in his walk-in closet. Japanese soaking tubs are all the rage in the design and architecture magazines so I'm not surprised Bethany wanted one."

"Sounds like she's a woman with expensive tastes."

"You were in the Cartwright house. That's putting it mildly. Tracy seemed to think Ben had reached his limit. She implied that if Bethany hadn't gotten pregnant, the marriage might be over. Maybe Ben was meeting with his divorce attorney last night and didn't want Bethany to know so he arranged a meeting late at night where no one would see him." Unnecessary and theatrical? Probably, but who's to say what a person would do when there's a lot of money involved.

Bartlett's response was a half-hearted grunt.

"You have a different theory?"

He was working on one. I could tell from the way he stared at his plate with his brows knit like he was studying a chessboard. Jim used to wear the same expression whenever he brought work home.

"When I spoke with her this morning, Bethany mentioned that Ben had been distracted lately. Could be she was preemptively covering up their problems, but… Arguing over expenditures. Cutting off his ex's alimony payments." He quirked an eyebrow. "Sounds like someone needed to economize."

"You think Ben was having money issues?"

Happened all the time. Developers overleveraged and found themselves upside down in debt when the market stalled.

"Tracy had said Ben used his money to keep the family close. "Maybe someone didn't like hearing they were about to be cut off. Years spent dancing to someone else's tune, only to find out you were going to be shortchanged would piss me off."

"Exactly," Bartlett replied. "The question is, was someone angry enough to kill?"

6

———

THE LAST WAKE I attended was Mary Lou Paretsky's, a sparsely attended affair that reflected the life she'd lived. In contrast, Ben Cartwright's wake was standing room only. A line of mourners stretched down the sidewalk. Half the town had to be in attendance. Proof that money could buy popularity.

"How much do you want to bet half these people came tonight hoping for family drama?" Rob asked as we took our place in line. In a sea of somber colors, he still managed to stand out with his ridiculously sumptuous cashmere topcoat and a plaid scarf that brought out the silver flecks in his hair. Precisely the kind of casual display of wealth that Ben Cartwright spent his life trying to achieve. If dead people could be jealous, Ben's spirit had to be seething.

For once, I'd attempted to match Rob's elegance, or at least not look too poor in comparison. I ditched my puffer coat for my camel hair trench and the water-colored scarf Tim gave me for Christmas. Rob commented on the outfit when I picked him up. We'd decided to carpool so neither of us would have to stand in line alone. "Very nice," he said. "I'm sure Cartwrights will appreciate the effort. Not to mention Dan Bartlett."

I'd tried to swat his good arm then, but he dodged out of the way. "I am not trying to impress Dan Bartlett," I said. "Just thought I'd get some wear out of this coat, is all."

"And the boots and skirt? I suppose they needed wear as well?"

I told him we were running late. Honestly, a girl couldn't put effort into her appearance with someone making a big deal about it.

Back in the line, Rob and I slowly made our way through the front door and into the crowded hallway. They'd removed the dividing wall that usually stood between the viewing rooms, but it didn't make much difference. People were still shoulder to shoulder. A thick smell of perfume clogged the air, and I wondered why there wasn't a law against overdoing floral scents.

I scanned the crowd for Bartlett. He'd texted to tell me what time he would be attending which, by coincidence, was the same time as Rob and me. He always attended crime victims' wakes. To reassure the dead that they would get justice, he once told me. No sign of his broad shoulders. Nor was the back of my neck tingling, which it always seemed when he was close. To my horror, I was disappointed.

An extra coat rack had been set up to accommodate the crowd. Seeing the black coats jammed together, I was glad I switched coats. The odds of taking home the wrong one were high. We watched as a woman tried three times before locating the right coat. "And you wonder why I refuse to wear one," Rob whispered.

Ben lay at the front of the room with a blanket of

white roses draped over his casket and his family in line on his right. To my surprise, Patty stood in the receiving line as well, wedged between Tracy and Kim. I could only guess the girls requested she stay with them for emotional support. Kim certainly looked like she needed it. While Tracy was clear-eyed and somber, Kim looked like the dead walking. A pair of oversized sunglasses shielded her eyes and cheeks and there were specks of white on the front of her dress, residue from the wad of tissues she was twisting back and forth. When people spoke, she nodded in that dull way someone who's been medicated would move. I'd been the same at Jim's funeral. The numbness had made the platitudes more bearable. Of the two girls, Kim had always been the closest to her father. Now she grieved the hardest.

I watched as Patty whispered something in her ear, then frowned when Kim shook her head. Attempting to make Kim sit down, maybe? The girl looked like she could use a break.

Interestingly, Steve, Kim's husband, didn't seem to notice his wife's distress. His focus was on Bethany. He hovered over Ben's widow like a giant bear. Although to be fair, Bethany *was* pregnant. I could see where, in her condition, she might need some looking after. Goodness knows Tracy wouldn't volunteer, given how much she disliked her stepmother.

"Hard to imagine one of them being a killer," Rob remarked. He'd read my mind. The five of them looked genuinely distraught, the way you'd expect a family shocked by a loved one's sudden death to look.

Bethany smiled sadly when we approached. Her fatigue was obvious despite the concealer caked beneath her eyes. "Thank you for coming. I know Ben would appreciate it."

How many times had she said that sentence?

"I work with Renee," I said. "She's out of town, but she asked me to tell you how sorry she is about Ben. He was a big personality. The town won't be the same without him."

"He was larger than life, wasn't he? He'd be thrilled to see how many people came to his wake. Nothing he liked better than a big audience. And Rob…" She leaned in to kiss his cheek. "I'm so glad to see you. Thank you for coming."

"Bethany helped decorate my house." She talked me out of using chintz in the dining room," Rob explained. "Told me Woodbridge is not the Cotswolds."

He clasped her hands. "How are you holding up?"

"Holding up. I keep needing to remind myself that Ben's really gone." Her fingers fluttered to her midsection and the small baby bump that protruded from beneath her knit dress. "The baby's what's keeping me going. Every time he moves, it's like Ben saying, 'I'm still here.'"

A beautiful sentiment that sounded very rehearsed.

"I keep telling her she needs to take care of herself. Getting run down isn't good for the baby," Steve said.

"Steve's appointed himself my personal mother hen. Reminding me to eat and stay hydrated. He's been a godsend."

"I'm only doing what Ben would want me to do," Steve replied. "I'm the only man left in the family now, and it's only right that I step up. He'd want someone looking after his child."

"You mean children, don't you?"

A second passed before my question registered on Steve's face. He looked to the end of the line where his wife stared into space like a zombie. If she was aware of the conversation, she was doing a great job of hiding it. "Right, children. Sorry. My mind's mush right now.

Between trying to keep people from panicking about Ben's death and the police…"

"I'm sure it's been hard on all of you," Rob said.

"An absolute nightmare," Bethany said. "Bad enough I've lost Ben, but we've got to deal with the police and all their awful questions. Was Ben worried about money? Were Ben and I unhappy? What kind of question is that? I'm pregnant, for crying out loud."

Being pregnant didn't always equal happy, a fact I'm sure Bartlett pointed out. "I know it's difficult, all those personal questions, but the police are only doing their job. They need to consider every angle—even the unlikely ones —if they want to catch Ben's murderer."

"If you ask me, they should chase down that crazy ex-secretary of his instead of harassing his family," Steve said.

"You mean Delfina?"

"She was obsessed," Bethany replied. "Always following him around. Parking her car outside our house at all hours of the night. She even showed up at Ben's birthday party! Said she wanted to 'wish him a happy birthday.'"

I remembered. She'd come to the restaurant with a birthday card. Bethany hadn't been happy.

"I wanted to get a restraining order, but Ben wouldn't hear of it. Said he would handle the situation. We argued about it after dinner that night. He told me to leave it alone so I said 'in that case, you can sleep alone," and went to the guest bedroom. That was the last time…" Her lower lip started to quiver.

"You didn't know. You couldn't have known," Steve said. He wrapped a comforting arm around her shoulder, but not before shooting a stern look at Rob and me.

Taking the hint, we moved down the line and offered our condolences first to Tracy and then to Patty and Kim.

"Thank you," Patty answered. "It's been a trying week for sure."

"For some, more than others," Tracy murmured.

"Leave your sister alone. You know how close she was to her father."

"Sorry."

"It's all right, honey. I know you're tired. It's been a long day. Another hour or so and we can put our feet up." She took the girls by the hand and gave them each a squeeze. A little maternal reassurance that everything would be okay. "Do you think you can handle another hour, Kim?"

Kim didn't answer.

Poor kids. I didn't care how cool Tracy played things, Ben was a big part of her life, and she would miss his presence. Both would. "Dan Bartlett's a good detective. He'll track down Ben's killer."

"Does he have any suspects?" Patty asked.

"Wouldn't surprise me," Rob said. "Not much gets by him. If he doesn't have a suspect in mind, you can bet he will soon."

Before either of us could say more, Kim let a low moan and collapsed into Rob's arms.

Quickly, we hustled her into a side room where she could compose herself. There she sat, with her head between her knees, while Tracy rubbed circles on her back. Rob volunteered to keep people from coming in, partially I think, to escape the hysterics.

Interestingly, Steve had remained in the receiving line.

"Don't," Patty said when I tried to apologize. "It's my fault. I should have told her to stay home. Kim's always been more... fragile than the rest of us. She feels things more deeply. Ben..." She offered a sad half-smile. "She was Ben's little princess. I remember when the girls were little, she was terrified of sleeping in the dark. Ben would make a big show of checking under her bed for monsters and pretending to chase them away. 'No one eats my princess,' he'd say in this stupid growl."

The smile faded. "Can't picture it, can you?"

"Not really, but people are always different with their children than the rest of the world." Growing up, my dad used to give me piggyback rides. I'd climb on his broad back, and pretend he was a wild pony I needed to tame. He'd buck me and toss me around until my stomach hurt from laughing. Then the phone would ring, and he'd need to check on his latest drug shipment.

"Yeah," Patty said, "Ben might have been a bastard, but he loved his girls. Even Tracy, although they haven't— hadn't— seen eye to eye in years. That's my fault too. I should've done a better job of shielding her from her father's infidelities, but she always was observant, and Ben could be careless."

"You mean Bethany wasn't the first time?"

"She wasn't even the second. It's a wonder Ben knew how to work a zipper; his fly was open so much. Bethany was simply the final straw."

Wow. I was stunned. I shouldn't have been. Ben had always considered himself a Top Dog, and Top Dogs didn't think rules applied to them. "I'm surprised you stayed as long as you did."

"What can I say? In a weird way, we worked. Business- wise we made a good team. And he was a good father. I didn't want the girls growing up in a broken home. I did, and it sucked."

"So you looked the other way."

"I looked the other way," she repeated.

A few feet away, Tracy and Kim had their heads together, talking softly. Kim was still shaky, but better.

Patty's eyes shimmered with tears. "The lengths a mother will go to protect her babies, huh?"

"Tell me about it," I said. We were all self-appointed martyrs, willing to sacrifice anything if it meant our child's happiness. "Who would have guessed labor was the easy part?" I was only half-joking, but we laughed anyway.

Patty ended hers with a sigh. "Then they grow up and make mistakes that aren't so easy to fix."

She didn't elaborate, but I had a feeling she was referring to her son-in-law, the new head of the family who still hadn't checked on his wife.

I was about to ask when the back of my neck began tingling. I turned around and saw Dan Bartlett standing in the doorway, hands clasped behind his back, waiting for permission to enter. "Everything all right?" His head nodded toward Kim.

"Everything's fine, Detective Bartlett. It's been a long week. Is there something you need?" Patty's spoke with accentuated formalness. It was 180 degrees from how she'd sounded before. Her posture was rigid, too. Apparently, Bethany wasn't the only one upset with Dan and his questioning.

"I wanted to offer my condolences," Dan said. "And to assure you that we're doing everything we can to find your ex-husband's killer."

"Thank you. Now, if you'll excuse me…"

"Of course. Again, I'm sorry for your loss. In the meantime, if any of you should remember anything new about that night—"

"I doubt there's anything we can add that we haven't already told you," Patty said.

"You never know. Even the smallest piece of information can make the difference."

"Mama?"

To our surprise, Kim was sitting up. Clutching a chintz throw pillow, she looked like a broken porcelain doll. "Would you take me home? I don't think I can deal…" She looked over her shoulder at the wall dividing us from the viewing room. From her husband and Bethany.

In a flash, Patty was at her side, brushing the hair from her daughter's face. "Sure, sweetheart. Why don't I take you both home? The two of you can rest up for tomorrow."

"I'll get the coats," Tracy announced.

A few minutes later, we watched the trio make their way past the line and out the door. "First Bethany and Steve Cho. Now Patty and the girls. The Cartwright family doesn't seem like you very much, Detective Bartlett," Rob remarked. "I wonder why?"

"So do I," Bartlett replied. "So do I."

7

"You know for a Cartwright gathering, this has been surprisingly drama-free," Rob remarked as we buttoned our coats. Having successfully chased away half the Cartwright family, the three of us decided it was time we left as well. The wake was nearly over anyway. The line was gone, and the crowd had thinned to a handful of patchy clumps.

"Other than Kim collapsing in despair," I said.

"That doesn't count. Kimberly's always been high-strung."

How did he know? I was going to ask when I noticed Bartlett had turned back to the viewing room. Following his gaze, I saw he was watching Bethany and Steve who were standing at Ben's coffin. She had her head bent while he rested a hand on her shoulder.

Bartlett appeared by my shoulder. "Cozy aren't they? The young, grieving widow and her devoted son-in-law praying over her dead husband."

"While his wife is home falling apart with grief." I

shook my head. Ten to one Ben's death wasn't the only thing causing Kim to fall apart. "He claims he's doing what Ben would want and looking after her."

"Told me the same thing."

"Do you buy it?"

"Sure. Just like I believed my partner when he said my wife and he were only friends."

We exchanged looks. Tracy was right. There was trouble at home.

"What do you know about the son-in-law?" Bartlett waited until we were outside before he asked the question.

"Beyond the fact he works for Ben, not much," I said. He didn't generate gossip like others in the family. Until tonight, I'd considered him and Kim the least dramatic ones in the family.

"Working with Ben is how he met Kimberly," Rob said. "She answered phones there while she was in college."

That reminded me. Rob was the second person at the wake to mention Kim's emotional fragility. "You called Kim high-strung. Why?"

"I had her as a student before she transferred to UMass. Cried her way through a couple of my lectures. Boyfriend problems, probably. I make it a rule not to ask when it happens. I've got enough drama in me life without theirs, too."

Bartlett stopped walking. "Your students cry a lot?"

"Romance poetry and a class full of sensitive students? Happens every other semester," Rob replied. He looked at me. "Kimberly didn't just cry; she sobbed. Big heaving sobs that made it impossible to concentrate."

"In other words, she's as dramatic as the rest of her family." Bartlett resumed walking.

"Not necessarily," Rob said. "Dramatic implies you

want attention. I never got the impression that her break-downs were anything other than breakdowns."

"Huh. Interesting."

"Interesting how?" I asked. Whenever Bartlett was chewing on an idea his voice took on this vague, distant tone. Whenever he used it, I was compelled to pull the information out of him. Sometimes he'd play along; some-times he wouldn't. I hoped he was in the mood to play.

"Well… That's odd."

I turned to see what caught Bartlett's attention. Although it was dark, Stillman's parking lot was brightly lit. A personal injury case a decade earlier caused the owners to install spotlights everywhere. In their glow, I saw Patty Cartwright deep in conversation with a stranger wearing a hooded coat. "I thought she was in a hurry to get home?"

"Me too." He stared harder, his frown growing more pronounced. "I've seen that coat before," he said.

"No surprise there," Rob replied.

"No, I mean I've seen *that coat* before. With that yellow scarf."

Now that he mentioned it, so had I. Delfina had been wearing the same coat and scarf combination when she visited Gilroy's on the night of the murder. "Bethany claimed Delfina was stalking them. Why would she be talking to Patty?"

"That's what I'd like to know," Bartlett replied.

Whatever the reason, Patty didn't look like she was enjoying the conversation. Twice she turned to open her car door only to have the other woman block her path. "Too bad we parked on the street, or we'd have an excuse to eavesdrop," Rob said.

Bartlett grinned. "You two might have parked on the street, but I didn't." With that, he stepped over the low boxwood border that divided the lot from the sidewalk and headed toward his car. Rob and I tossed each other a quick look before following suit.

The women's conversation looked heated. Delfina had arms positioned on either side of Patty's body, pinning her in place. Through the windshield, I could see Kim and Tracy watching with wide eyes.

"Is everything okay?" Bartlett called out.

The pair froze. "We're fine, Detective," Patty called out.

"Yes, just catching up," Delfina added. She'd backed away, the increased space allowing Patty to, finally, open her driver's door. "I was telling Patty a funny story. About Ben. One she hadn't heard."

So funny Patty didn't want to hear it. Now that Bartlett had interrupted, she wasted no time in getting into her car and shutting the door. Delfina spoke to her through the glass. "Nice talking with you, Patty. I'll call you tomorrow." After waving Patty off, she headed toward the driveway at the rear of the lot.

"That's her!" Bethany's voice rang across the night. Ben's widow was leaning over the porch railing, pointing at Delfina. "That's the crazy witch who's been stalking us! Someone stop her!"

"You're the witch," Delfina shouted back. "Whoring around behind Ben's back. I hope you rot in hell."

"You rot in hell!"

"No one is going to rot anywhere," Bartlett's sharp voice killed the back and forth. "Not tonight anyway. Mrs. Cartwright, go back into inside. Delfina, I'm going to need you to come with me."

Delfina shook her head. "Not tonight."

It was a chain reaction after that. Delfina started walking away when Bethany, who had ignored Bartlett's instructions and remained outside, started screaming again. "Don't let her go! She killed my husband!"

Steve Cho leaped over the porch railing and charged toward Delfina. Bartlett stopped him, but Delfina fled anyway. We heard a horn. Screeching brakes. Then a voice.

"Call 9-1-1!"

8

———

IT WAS LATE when Rob and I—and Dan Bartlett—dragged ourselves up Rob's front steps and into his gourmet kitchen. Talk about a night. In running from Steve, Delfina had run straight into the path of an SUV. The driver said Delfina appeared so unexpectedly that despite slamming on his brakes, he couldn't stop in time. Witnesses said she flew up and over the car's hood, before landing like a rag doll on the pavement.

Her prognosis wasn't good. Even if she survived, doctors weren't sure what her condition would be.

"The two of you didn't have to stay," Bartlett said as followed us through the front door. As one of the first on the scene, he'd had to provide a statement to the responding officer before heading to the hospital to check on Delfina's condition. Rob and I had tagged along to keep him company. We didn't feel right abandoning him, and though Bartlett didn't say anything aloud, we could tell he appreciated the gesture. For all his gruffness, Bartlett had a sensitive soul. Tim told me how long he would take to interview victims, making sure they were comfortable before asking difficult questions.

"We wanted to," Rob told him.

"Besides," I added, "it gave me a chance to check out Rob's new boyfriend." I'd recognized him the minute he arrived on the scene. Not too many EMTs looked like Anderson Cooper.

"Stop calling him my boyfriend. He's a good friend and nothing more."

"A good friend who eats eggs at two in the morning," I whispered over my shoulder. Bartlett flashed his first grin in hours.

"Oi! I heard that," Rob said. "Tell you what, I'll talk when you two talk."

Bartlett and I shut up.

In the kitchen, we discovered Eliot, one of Rob's cats, sleeping in what looked like a nest of satin on the counter.

"Bad kitty. You know you're not to be up here." Rob scooped up the tabby and cuddled her, heedless of the hair she would leave on his dark suit. "We don't sleep on the counters."

"Might sound more threatening if you weren't kissing him on the head," I said.

"Like you don't kiss your cat's head."

"Not when he's misbehaving, I don't."

"You two sound like crazy people, you know that, don't you?" Bartlett remarked.

Dog person, I mouthed to Rob. Bartlett reached over and picked up the item Eliot had turned into his bed. It was a satin baseball jet. Metallic gold with cherry red trim and piping. "Is this?"

"One of me old RU Ready jackets," Rob replied, his voice a mixture of pride and chagrin. "Theresa is starting a paraphernalia display for the band."

Theresa Crowe had recently purchased a house in Rob's neighborhood, a cute little ranch whose owner had her head smashed with a frying pan. As someone obsessed with true crime, Theresa loved the idea of owning an actual murder home. It was she who provided the key piece of evidence that cleared Rob's name. Rob had been trying to ingratiate himself with her ever since.

There was one problem, though. Theresa was crazy.

"Are we talking about Theresa who's in love with the imaginary detective?" Bartlett asked.

Rob stopped him with a raised finger. "Christopher Grimes of *Grimes on the Street* is not imaginary; he is a modern-day Sherlock Holmes and the two of them connect through lucid dreaming."

"My mistake. I didn't realize we were talking lucid dreaming…" The sentence drifted into a yawn. Between Delfina's accident and Ben's wake, it'd been a long night.

Rob reached into the cupboard and handed Bartlett a tin of peppermint tea, then opened the wine. Together we sat in comfortable silence listening to the hissing of water boiling in the kettle. Bartlett's knee rested against mine, the contact intimate and reassuring. Swirling my wine, I watched the red splash against the sides of the glass and replayed the night. If only Delfina hadn't run.

"Stupid Steven Cho," I muttered. If he hadn't frightened Delfina away…

"From the look on his face, I bet he'll think twice before playing hero again," Rob said.

Too bad he hadn't thought twice this time.

What were she and Patty talking about? Had Ben's ex-wife discovered her stalking the wake? Then why did it look like Delfina was the aggressor? "Do you think Bethany could be right?" I asked. "That Delfina shot Ben?"

"Possibly. What do you two know about her?"

I took a moment to breathe in the peppermint aroma rising from his mug before answering. "Not much. She was pleasant and easy to deal with. I didn't have to speak slowly for her to understand. Some of Ben's secretaries were——"

"Dumb as posts," Rob supplied.

"Vapid would be a better word," I said. "They could have been smart, but somewhere along the line figured out the fiscal benefits of being stupid. Know what I mean?"

"Ben liked them pretty and shallow."

Rob raised his glass in a mock toast. "Exactly. He just got lucky with Delfina. I saw them together once. Having dinner at a restaurant in Worcester."

"Bit of a drive or a business dinner," Bartlett noted.

"This isn't the kind of place you go to a business dinner. Unless business dinners have changed, and people drink champagne at them now."

Not at any of the meetings I ever attended. We were lucky if Renee sprung for coffee and doughnuts. I remembered something. "Patty did say Ben slept around a lot when they were married. Sounds like Delfina might have been one of his conquests."

"Only to be replaced by another 'secretary.' Which" — Bartlett paused to take a swallow of tea— "explains why she was hanging around, 'stalking' as Bethany put it. She didn't take the break-up well."

"Heaven has no rage, like love to hatred turned, Nor hell a fury, like a woman scorned," Rob quoted over the rim of his glass.

Another piece of the puzzle clicked in for me. The note on Ben's passenger seat. "The night of the murder. She gave Ben an envelope. At the time, I thought it was a birthday card, but what if it was also a note asking to meet her later? They meet, she begs for another chance, and she shoots him in the back as he's walking away."

"Only one problem," Rob said. "Why go to the bother of saying no in person when ignoring the note would do the same trick?"

"He'd have to have a reason to meet her," Bartlett said. "Money? Blackmail?"

Bartlett shook his head. "She wouldn't get much. We checked into Cartwright's finances. He was massively overextended. No wonder he was looking to cut expenses."

"Like Patty's alimony," I said.

Rob sighed. "Poor Patty. Bad enough Cartwright screwed around while they were married, but to screw her after the divorce? When she's the reason you're rich? Takes stones, that does."

"Big ones," I said with a yawn.

It was late, and my eyelids were getting heavy. Red wine after midnight might not have been the best idea. Left me cozy and sleepy. I was about to ask Rob if I could crash in his guest room when a shrill ring made us all jump.

"This can't be good," Bartlett said as he reached into his breast pocket. "It's the station." My heart automatically jumped to my throat as soon as he said the words.

"Tim's not working tonight, is he?" Rob asked after Bartlett moved into the living room to talk.

I shook my head. Tim was the first person I thought of every time there was a late-night phone call. Thankfully, he was working the day shift, and since he hated working without enough sleep, had probably been asleep for hours. In high school, he was the only teenager who insisted on turning his light out before midnight, a habit that became more ingrained as he grew older. My heart settled back into place.

"Maybe it's an update on Delfina," I said. Hopefully a positive one. There were a lot of questions that she had the answers to. At the top of the list: why was she confronting Patty in the parking lot?

"What are you doing tomorrow?" I asked.

"Teaching. Why?" Rob frowned at me with suspicion in his eyes. "What are you planning?"

"I thought I might stop by Patty's house after Ben's funeral. If Delfina can't answer our questions, maybe Patty will."

"Because she was so forthcoming in the parking lot tonight." Bartlett had asked her to stick around while the police gathered witness statements, but Patty refused. Kim was too distraught to stay, she claimed.

"Because it was Bartlett who asked. For some reason she doesn't like him," I said. "But she does like us. Maybe a friendly face might prod her into sharing more."

"So much for not being involved," he said.

I shrugged. What could I say? I couldn't help myself. Some people can't resist sugar, I couldn't resist a crime. "Do you want to come with me?" I asked.

Sighing, he raised his glass to drink the last of its contents. "Why the hell not?"

"That was the station," Bartlett repeated as he strode back into the kitchen, a somber expression on his face. "Patty Cartwright just turned herself in."

9

I DIDN'T UNDERSTAND. Turned herself in for what?

"Killing her ex-husband," Bartlett said. "She walked into the station about fifteen minutes ago and announced she shot Ben."

Wow. Talk about unexpected. Made sense though. She certainly had a motive. Beyond the business with the alimony, Ben had been screwing her for years. Screwing around on her and screwing her. I imagined enduring decades of slights, each one adding another layer of anger that she tamped down for their daughters' sake. You can only swallow rage for so long before it becomes too much. Like pressure in a bottle, it builds and builds until the top blows off.

"Guess we know what Delfina wanted now," Rob said. "She was confronting Patty about the crime. Urging her to confess. Wonder if Delfina's accident is what pushed Patty into talking tonight? Guilt over an innocent person getting hurt?"

"Something pushed her into showing up." Bartlett

pushed his mug across the counter. "Thanks for the tea. I needed it."

I caught his arm. "Wait. Are you going to talk with Patty *now*?"

"Unless she's asked for a lawyer, yes."

I got to my feet and reached for my coat. This time Bartlett caught my arm. "What are you doing?"

"Going to the station." I wanted to hear Patty's answers as much as he did.

"I didn't realize you'd joined the police force, Detective McIntyre."

The patronizing note in his voice went right up my back. "Very funny."

"It wasn't a joke." Then, as if he couldn't be annoying enough, he tucked a knuckle under my chin and lifted my face, forcing me to look him straight on.

"Look," he said. "While I appreciate everything you and Rob have done to this point, your role ends here. Let the police—let me—do my job. Okay?"

When I didn't answer, he leaned closer, his face hovering inches from mine. "Okay?" he repeated.

Like I had a choice. "Okay," I muttered.

"Thank you. I'll call you in the morning."

I don't know if it was the proximity or if he forgot we weren't alone, but he dipped his head and kissed me. Short and sweet, like he kissed me goodbye all the time. I considered frowning, but it's hard to feel annoyed when your lips taste like peppermint. By the time I managed to react, Bartlett had shrugged on his jacket and let himself out, so I glared at Rob and his overly amused grin. "Don't say a word," I said.

"About the goodbye kiss? Wouldn't dream of it. Refill?"

Why not? I handed him my glass, any lingering thoughts of driving home effectively erased. I still can't believe Patty is the one who shot Ben. She seemed so composed."

"Was this before or after Kimberly collapsed?"

Okay, maybe composed was the wrong word. In command. Of the situation, of herself. "Before. I mean, way before. When I saw her the morning after the murder. Sad, yes, but in control. You would never have guessed that twelve hours before she'd shot her ex-husband in the back."

"Don't know why you're surprised. None of the other murderers we've met acted suspicious either." He set down the bottle with a clunk. "I can't believe I just used those words in normal conversation."

Neither could I. Ironic, wasn't it? Running from my dangerous family only to land in a town where murders took place as often as soccer matches. He had a point though. None of the killers acted suspiciously. That is, until they panicked and slipped up. Usually that meant killing again. In Patty's case, it led to a late-night confession.

The late hour. I had this odd, niggling sensation in my stomach, and that was the reason. What made Patty feel she had to rush in and confess tonight? The police weren't going anywhere. Why not wait until morning? Or better yet, after Ben's funeral so she could support her daughters, the way she did at the wake?

I posed the question to Rob, who shrugged. "My guess? Delfina threatened to go to the police if she didn't."

"But that was before Delfina had her accident. Even if Delfina did threaten to talk, wouldn't you wait to learn whether the woman survived or not before turning yourself in?"

"Unless she felt partially responsible for the accident, and her guilty conscience compelled her to talk. One body too many or something."

"Still doesn't explain why she rushed to confess tonight."

"You know what I think? I think that *you're* overthinking. Murderers don't adhere to the same logic as normal people. Patty confessed. End of story."

Was it the end? The evidence certainly said so.

Why, I wondered as I sipped my wine, did my gut feel like we were missing something?

———

WHEN TIM MOVED BACK to Woodbridge after college, I was surprised. Having spent years girding my loins for his inevitable departure, I never expected him to live five miles away. A guilty part of me suspected his sticking close had to do with me being a widow, but a bigger, more guilty part was elated. Determined not to blow this unexpected gift, I vowed not to be overly involved in his life—the mother who gave her son space. *Set the bird free and he'll fly back*, the saying goes.

To that end, I suggested a semi-monthly dinner date. Every two weeks, Tim plopped himself at my kitchen island, ate a homecooked meal, and told me absolutely nothing about his personal life. Just like high school, only now he didn't have to sneak the beer.

I hosted such a dinner the night following Patty's confession. Tim arrived annoyed over, believe it or not, birthday cake.

"She baked a cake. Can you believe it? Everyone else picks up a couple of packs of cupcakes or grabs doughnuts when it's someone's birthday, but no, she had to make a chocolate cake. With homemade frosting."

The object of his wrath was the newest member of the force, a cute little blond named Brooke Hobbs. She joined the force after the New Year and became Tim's nemesis shortly after. *Brooke showed him up. Brooke didn't get the same hazing he did. Brooke flirted with the dispatcher.*

He'd complained the same way about Becky Costello in seventh grade. Two years later, I caught them kissing on the porch.

When he paused to drink his beer, I took advantage of the silence and changed the subject. "May I ask you a question? If you publicly threatened a person, would you turn around and shoot him the same night?"

Tim grinned over his bottle. "You're talking about the Cartwright murder, aren't you? Uncle Rob warned me you weren't letting it go."

How helpful of him. I'd have to be sure to say thank you. "When did you see Rob?"

"This afternoon at the liquor store. He stopped to tell me he wasn't coming tonight. I didn't know he was dating Sean O'Donnell."

"Who?"

"EMT. Looks like Anderson Cooper. The two of them were debating red wine choices."

"So that's his name. Rob says they aren't, but the evidence says otherwise." Speaking of evidence… "Getting back to my question. Would you?"

I waited while he took another swallow. "Short answer? Yes. Witnesses said Mrs. Cartwright publically threatened her ex-husband.. Not a huge leap to think she decided to follow through."

Bartlett said the same thing when he called that morning. As he predicted, Patty's lawyer shut down any further conversation meaning answers would have to wait. But based on what little Patty said before he arrived, Bartlett had a pretty good idea of how the night unfolded.

"Thing is," I said, "Patty was angry about Ben *cutting*

her alimony. She wanted Ben to keep paying which he can't do if he's dead. Wouldn't killing him be shooting herself in the foot—no pun intended?"

"She wouldn't need Ben to pay. Her daughters inherited half of his estate. She probably assumed they'd take care of her."

"Assuming there was much of an estate to inherit. Ben was broke."

"In that case, she had nothing to lose."

Nothing but her freedom if she got caught. My timer went off meaning my pork loin was done. As much as I adored Italian cooking, I stopped making spaghetti in favor of healthier, more balanced meals.

As I set the roast on the platter to sit before carving, I worked through the events leading up to Ben's killing. I couldn't let go of the feeling we'd missed a dot in the connect-the-dots. "So, Patty left the restaurant, decided enough was enough, and she was going to have it out with Ben once and for all. At gunpoint, to keep him from walking away. She goes home and gets a gun... Where'd she get the gun?"

"She has a license to conceal carry. The whole family has licenses."

I stared at him. "The whole family? Even the girls?"

"It's a dangerous world, Ma. People want to protect themselves. You'd be surprised how many people in Woodbridge are walking around armed."

"Might be less... Never mind." We could go down the gun control rabbit hole another time. I wanted to figure out Patty's timeline. "Where's the gun now?"

"Said she tossed it in the Sudbury River."

How convenient, I thought.

"Okay, Patty has the gun. She goes to a store, buys a birthday card, scribbles out a meeting time, and... what?

How'd she deliver it? Slip it under his door? The security cameras would have caught her."

"Tucked it under his windshield at the restaurant." He appeared at my shoulder. "Oven-roasted potatoes?"

Took me a moment to realize he was asking about dinner. "Yes, and gravy. Sounds like a lot of work to set up a meeting."

"What should she have done? Texts and calls can be traced."

"Why a card, though? Why not scribble a note on a piece of paper?"

"Maybe she didn't have paper? Or maybe she didn't want people to know it was from her. I'm sure we'll find out once she makes her statement. Can we leave the potatoes in longer so they're extra crispy?"

The last part said while peering into the oven. He wanted to change the subject. Like Bartlett and Rob, as long as they had their killer, the loose ends didn't bother him.

I wish I felt the same.

10

The card had a bright yellow envelope.

The memory came to me just as I was falling asleep. The birthday card lying on Ben's front seat on top of a yellow envelope. Both creased down the middle as if folded in half. Like a person would do if they wanted to stuff it in a smaller space. I'd seen that envelope before.

My thoughts dialed back to the restaurant. Delfina. The card she gave Ben had a yellow envelope. Ben put it in his back pocket.

After he folded it in half.

Patty hadn't arranged the meeting at the playground; Delfina had. Ben had gone there to talk with his former secretary. About what? And how did Patty find out?

Fully awake by this point, I grabbed my cell phone from my nightstand and started texting.

11

"Good question," Bartlett said when I asked him the next morning. We were sitting in my car enjoying breakfast while I waited for a client to arrive for a showing. My car smelled of warm sugar, coffee, Old Spice, and mint, a delectable combination that air freshener companies wished they could duplicate. "According to her statement, she waited outside Ben's house, saw him leave, and followed."

"At two a.m.? How did she know Ben was planning to go out?"

"I asked her that." Of course, he had. Bartlett never overlooked details. "The answer is, she didn't. She planned to wait near the house so she could intersect Ben on his way to work. Ben going to the park was purely coincidental."

"All night in the middle of February? Seemed a bit over the top."

"I asked her that too. She said she wasn't thinking straight." *No kidding.*

Bartlett pointed to the house, a 3000-square foot Colonial with a pool, with his cup. "Out of curiosity, how much would something like this sell for?"

"Too much," I replied. And definitely out of reach on a cop's salary. This was Ben Cartwright country. Expensive homes for people with big incomes where dairy cows once grazed. "There's a townhouse coming on the market next week I think will be perfect for you."

Bartlett nodded. "Do you sell a lot of these? Gigantic houses, that is?"

"Some," I said. Luxury homes were more Renee's area. "They aren't selling like they used to, though. Prices have jumped too much for the average homebuyer."

"And Ben was knee-deep in properties like these? No wonder he was cutting costs."

Such was the rollercoaster of real estate development. It was hard to feel sorry for Ben, though. He knew the risk. Poor Bethany could be in for a surprise. Imagine thinking you married a millionaire and inheriting a mound of debt instead. I wondered how her new white knight, Steve Cho, would feel. Both Bethany and his wife could be inheriting less than expected.

While I was busy thinking about the Cartwright finances, a comfortable silence settled over the car. Bartlett and I sipped our drinks, content to watch a flock of turkeys as it crossed the front yard. "Did you know," I said as the birds turned down the driveway, "that when I first moved to Woodbridge, you barely saw turkeys. Now they're everywhere, like giant suburban pigeons. They don't even fear people anymore."

"This group seems right at home, that's for sure. Do they come with the property?"

"Let's hope not," I said. "Have you ever tried to get out of your car when there's a turkey nest nearby? One spring

I had to carry a wiffle ball bat with me. Mama turkeys don't mess around."

"Never met a mother who did when it came to protecting her baby." He flashed me a smile. "Remind me to watch my back if I ever have to fire Tim."

"Absolutely." While I grinned, I was only partially joking. After all, I'd already moved heaven and earth to protect him. "Never underestimate what a mother will do for her child."

The hairs on the back of my neck started rising. Something about that phrase…

———

IF I THOUGHT TALKING with Bartlett would answer the questions in my head, I was wrong. They were connected —Delfina's note and Patty's confession—I knew they were. Unlike Tracy Cartwright, I didn't believe in fortuitous coincidences. The question was, *how?*

The showing, by the way, was a disaster. The prospective buyers were snooty, and with all the stuff in my head, I didn't have it in me to show them the proper condescension. Plus, Bartlett went and kissed me goodbye again. I swear he used those peppermint-flavored pecks as a distraction technique. No way he didn't know their power.

Even Bartlett's kiss couldn't keep me from dwelling on Ben's final hours, though. As soon as the buyers' BMW pulled away, I was in my car jotting down what I knew.

First, Ben was having financial problems and trying to cut expenses. Second, he was being stalked by Delfina, or so Bethany believed. On the night of the murder, Patty claimed to also be stalking Ben.

The was an awful lot of stalking.

Finally, Delfina gave Ben a birthday card listing a time

and place for a meeting in the park. Why the park? And why in the middle of the night? If she wanted to confront him, why not go to his office the following morning? Seems a lot less complicated.

Unless…

What if Delfina wasn't asking for a meeting? What if she was relaying information about someone else's clandestine rendezvous? Like a young wife and her very chummy step-son-in-law?

A theory began forming in my head. One that explained everything.

It was time to have a chat with Bethany.

12

———————

Whether it was by coincidence or design, Ben Cartwright's house sat at the top of Ridge Road, the highest point in Woodbridge. I'm sure at some point, he realized that his property let him look down on the entire town, a discovery that must have given him great pleasure. Over the years, he'd expanded and modified the design, the house's grandiosity growing with his success. What started as a large Colonial was now a sprawling estate with an arched portico and massive custom windows.

Although Ben's house was the last one on the street, Ridge Road itself continued for several yards so larger vehicles could turn around. Plenty of room for a person to park and watch the comings and goings from Ben's driveway without notice.

In fact, I was idling on the side of the road when a black SUV exited the drive. For a second, I thought I was seeing ghosts. The burly silhouette on the other side of the tinted glass looked a lot like Ben. But it was only Steve Cho in his expensive black puffer coat. Guess with Ben dead and buried, he and Bethany didn't have a reason to hide.

Bethany answered the door in a cashmere lounge suit that managed to accent and camouflage her pregnancy bump simultaneously. Without makeup, she looked beautiful. Tired, but fresh-faced and glowing.

She gave me a withering look when I asked if we could talk. "Little soon to be asking if I'm putting the house on the market, isn't it?" she asked.

"This isn't about the house. It's about Ben."

"Ben? Why do you have questions about him?"

Good question. I launched into the excuse I'd drafted in my head during the drive across town. About how I'd been unable to stop thinking about everything that had happened. "It's difficult to comprehend," I told her. "Especially that mess with Delfina after the wake. I mean, I've known these people for years and had no idea how unhinged they were. Are. This is going to sound crazy, but I figured you might be having the same problem, and that if we could talk, we might be able to… I don't know, settle any loose ends that are bothering us."

I should have brought a casserole.

Bethany frowned. "Why? Patty's confessed. Who cares about loose ends?"

"What if Patty didn't do it?" I asked.

"*She confessed,*" Bethany replied. "She hated that Ben stopped the gravy train and got revenge."

"I'm not so sure that's true."

Her expression hardened. "You've got some nerve, you know that? I've heard people talk about you, about your amateur sleuthing, and I think it's incredibly insensitive to show up here the day after my husband's funeral peddling some lame story about loose ends. Patty Carmichael killed my husband. End of story. Now get off my property before I call the police."

I jammed my foot in the door. To hell with it, I

thought. She knew my reason for being there. Why not jump straight to the bluntness?

"Did Ben know about you and Steve?" I asked.

The color drained from her face. "Fine, you can come inside," she said.

No one would ever accuse Bethany of having bad taste. The interior was a study on the proper use of light and color, right down to the warm yellow bulbs in her chandelier. "This is gorgeous," I said. Gorgeous and expensive. Seeing it up close, Tracy's comment about the seven-K tub sounded very believable.

Bethany folded her arms above her belly. "What do you want?" she asked, sounding more like a no-nonsense super boss than a pregnant widow. Suddenly, I could see how she got Ben to marry her. The arrogant sucker had been battling a true operator.

I bounced up and down on my toes, hands stuffed in my pockets, and did my best to look unfazed. "Like I said, I want to tie up some loose ends."

"Such as?"

"Delfina."

"That crazy woman. What about her?"

"Well, for starters, she wasn't stalking Ben," I said. "They were having an affair."

"Don't be ridiculous. Her and Ben? No way."

Right, because both the proven adulterers in their marriage couldn't be unfaithful.

"They were seen together. And," I added before she could speak, "because of how Ben acted when he saw her at Gilroy's. He spoke to her calmly and softly. In fact, if I recall, he was more upset with you for talking about her than he was about her showing up at the restaurant. Weird behavior for a guy who berated the hostess for all the world to hear not five minutes earlier. Then there was the birthday card the police found in his car with the time and place written inside. The envelope matches the one Delfina gave him, including the crease where Ben stuffed it into his back pocket."

I had two theories to go with my facts. Theory one, Delfina set up a birthday rendezvous. Theory two, she was passing along information about someone else's rendezvous.

Bethany was a horrible actress. As soon as I mentioned theory two, she grew way too interested in toeing the marble tile. I got my answer.

"How long have the two of you been seeing each other?" I asked.

"Eight months. We were going to wait until after the baby was born before telling him. We didn't want Ben—"

"Cutting off any potential child support."

To her credit, she looked me in the eye when she nodded. Eight months meant she and Steve had been together long enough for him to have fathered her child. Once he discovered the affair, Ben would have wondered. "The baby could be Ben's," she said.

"And biracial. Not sure Ben would accept Ben, Jr. under those circumstances."

"We planned to cross that bridge when we got to it."

Would have been one heck of a bridge, I thought, but that didn't matter now. I was more interested in their hook-up plans and the second half of my theory.

"That night Delfina discovered your plans and told Ben when and where you were meeting in a birthday card in the hopes that he'd catch you in the act. How did you plan to sneak out without Ben knowing?" I'd been wondering ever since the murder. Two people living in the same house sneaking around in the middle of the night?

How'd they manage not to cross paths? Did these people not pay attention to one another?

"Easy," she replied. "I'd tell Ben the baby was giving me heartburn and go sleep in the spare bedroom. After a couple of Scotches, nothing woke him up. Doesn't matter though. We didn't go. Steve and Kim had this giant fight, and she went berserk. Screaming, crying—Kim is very good at hysterics in case you didn't know. *I won't let that woman steal you away*. That sort of thing."

That woman... "Are you saying Kim knew about the affair?"

Bethany waved off the question like it was no big deal. "Steve thinks she overheard us talking at the restaurant. Anyway, we'd already canceled because I didn't want to sit in the car in the middle of the night. Steve spent the night at the hotel. So, if you're trying to help your friend Patty out by suggesting Steve or I had something to do with Ben's murder, you're out of luck. We weren't there." She smiled.

"You realize that your story gives you an even stronger motive, don't you? If Kim told her father, you'd both be out on the street, but if Ben died before he could kick you out..." It was my turn to smile. Oddly enough, I believed her story. She was way too blasé about the details to be lying. I just wanted to wipe the satisfaction off her face.

"The desk clerk saw Steve, and my security footage shows I never left. Not that it matters since Patty—"

"She confessed. I know." As people were intent on reminding me.

The second half of my theory was coming together. There was only one more person to talk to. If I was right, then I knew exactly why Patty confessed to the crime.

13

———————

THE FIRST THING I did after leaving Bethany's house was pull out my phone to call Bartlett, only to find out that he'd texted me first.

> DB: Good news. D woke up. Heading to hosp now. Ttyl.

Good news indeed. The notion of Delfina never waking up had been weighing on me since the accident. No one deserved to languish like a vegetable. I said a little prayer for her continued recovery before turning to my less altruistic thought, that Delfina might be the one person besides Patty and Kim who could prove my theory.

"The lengths a mother will go to protect her babies…" That's what Patty had said at the wake. Look at me. I'd erased my entire existence for Tim's sake. How far would Patty go for her child?

Her fragile, emotional child.

I had too many thoughts in my head to work through alone. I called Rob. He was at Cuppas.

"I figured out why Patty confessed."

"What are you talking about? We know why she confessed. Because—"

"No, she didn't."

Quickly I filled him in, including the news about Delfina's condition and the birthday card. "Delfina found out where and when Bethany was meeting Steve and passed him the information at the restaurant."

"You mean like, 'Happy Birthday, lover. Here's some leverage for your divorce negotiations?'"

"Exactly." Although I wasn't sure how much leverage it provided considering Ben was cheating too, but I suppose that when you're broke, you'll try everything. "Only Bethany and Steve changed their plans and didn't go to the park."

"That explains why Ben was at the park, but what does it have to do with Patty?"

"Bethany told me that Steve and Kimberly had a huge fight the night Ben died and that Steve went to a hotel. One guess what the fight was about."

"Steve's relationship with his step-mother-in-law."

"Bingo. Turns out Ben and Delfina weren't the only ones who knew about the assignation. Kim did too. What if she decided to go to the park as well?"

"What if she did?" Rob said. "The only person there was her father— Wait, are you suggesting that Kim…?"

I was.

"Hear me out," I said. "Kim's overwrought. Hysterical. Her husband is leaving her for her stepmother. There's no way she's letting her husband walk out on her for Bethany. So, she grabs her gun—Tim said the whole family's armed—"

"The whole family?"

"It's a dangerous world, Rob. People want to protect themselves. Where was I?"

"Kim's got a gun."

"Right. Kim's a mess. She grabs her gun and drives to the park where she sees a man standing by the swing set who she thinks is her husband and, hysterical, shoots him in the back. Late at night and not thinking straight. Easy to see how she could confuse one guy in a black puffer coat for another."

There was silence on the other end of the line, then Rob whispered, "Bloody hell" again. "That's a hell of a theory, Sadie."

But it made sense. More so than Patty stalking her ex-husband following a fight. Kim was the emotional one in the family, the one prone to over-the-top reactions. Wasn't hard to believe she snapped that night, only to learn she'd shot her father by mistake. I couldn't imagine her grief and guilt when she learned the truth. No wonder Kim was beside herself.

"Delfina must have figured out the truth or thought she had," I said, "and that's why she confronted Patty at the wake. Then when it looked like Delfina wouldn't survive the accident—"

"Patty decided to confess and protect Kim from going to jail for a tragic mistake. Risky strategy."

True, but parents had done more for lesser reasons. And if she hired a sharp enough lawyer, Patty might wrangle herself a reduced sentence.

Of course, my theory would stay just that, a theory, without evidence. For that, I needed to talk with one more person.

"I'm on my way to Kim's house now to ask her a few questions," I told him. "If I'm right, hearing Delfina is awake might convince Kim to admit the truth."

"Shouldn't you wait for Bartlett?"

"Bartlett's at the hospital with Delfina. I left a message

for him to meet me. Besides," I added. "I'll be fine. We're talking about Kim. She's not a killer at heart."

"No, just an actual killer," he replied.

"Potentially," I reminded him. And even if she was the killer, what did he think she was going to do? Open the door holding a gun? I could handle a few minutes of conversation without Bartlett present.

I turned onto Appleton Way with its cookie-cutter colonials and tree-lined median. I'll say this about Ben's developments: what they lacked in architectural originality they made up for in family appeal. From the basketball hoops dotting every other driveway to the snow piled in the cul-de-sac, everything about the street screamed kid-friendly neighborhood.

Steve's black SUV was parked in the driveway when I arrived. Just what I needed. No way she would admit anything with him there. I needed to talk with her alone. I turned off the engine and settled in to wait.

That's when I noticed the foot in the doorway.

14

___

THE FOOT BELONGED to Steve Cho. He lay in the entrance, next to the stairs, blood running down the side of his face. A smashed wedding photo lay next to him.

I whipped out my phone.

"Don't bother," a voice said from above. "I already called."

Kim sat on the staircase above me, looking strangely put together. Hair blown out, makeup on. Her lipstick was on point. Not what I expected. She had something in her hands, but it wasn't her phone. That sat on the step next to her.

"What happened?" I asked.

She shrugged. "I killed him."

The cut on Steve's head didn't look serious enough to be fatal, despite the blood. I pressed my fingers to his neck. His pulse was strong and steady.

"He was leaving," Kim said. "To go back to *her*. I wasn't going to let him walk out this time."

"You mean like he did on Valentine's Day?"

Her sharp. laugh sounded more like a sob. "Valentine's

Day. Can't you believe it? What kind of man leaves his wife on Valentine's Day?"

"Same kind of guy who'd ignore his wife at her father's funeral," I said, and although I meant it—Steve Cho was a class-A jerk—I thought showing some solidarity might get her to talk.

"He said they were going to be a family. Him, Bethany, and the baby. What about our family? What about me?" She stared at her clasped hands. At whatever it was between her fingers. "It's all his fault. He never should have walked out. My dad would still be here if he'd stayed."

"Because then you'd have never gone to the playground," I said.

A shiver ran down my spine when Kim nodded. I was right. Patty *was* protecting her daughter. "It was supposed to be him," she said in a soft voice. "He was the one who was supposed to pay. I would never hurt Daddy."

I know. It was an accident." I saw this morning how similar the men were built. Easy to imagine a hysterical woman mistaking one shadowy figure for the other. "You didn't know your father was there."

"It was supposed to be Steve. I heard him talking with *her* at the restaurant about meeting in the park."

Only Bethany cancelled the plans. In the end, only Kim and her father, and maybe Delfina, kept the appointment.

"I confronted Steve when we got home," Kim was saying. "Asked him if there was something going on between him and Bethany. I was hoping he'd say it was all a crazy misunderstanding. Except he didn't."

She drew her legs closer to her body, trying to make herself smaller. "Do you know what he said?" He called her the love of his life. Her. The bimbo who seduced my father." For the first time since we began talking, she looked down at Steve's body. The man still hadn't moved. Was he playing dead until the EMTs arrived? "He used to say I was the love of his life, that we'd spend forever together, but he lied." Her face began to crumple. "Everything he promised was a lie."

"He and Bethany lied to your father, too. Ben went to the park that night to catch them."

"I didn't know," Kim whispered. "Poor Daddy. Steve should have been there instead of him."

"What happened?" I sked.

"Dad gave Tracy and I handguns for a present last Christmas. For self-protection. Steve laughed at the time. Said I was too delicate to use a firearm." The smallest of glimmers appeared in her eye. "Who's laughing now?" she asked.

So, she shows up angry and hysterical. Sees a dark figure by the swing set and shoots. That explained the murder, but what about Patty. "How did your mother find out?"

Kim let out a sigh. "The night of the wake. That crazy woman told my mother she saw the whole thing. Said if I didn't turn myself in, she'd tell the police everything. But then she got hit by the car."

And Patty, believing the only witness who could link Kim to the crime was dead, stepped up to take the blame.

"I took another Xanax and fell asleep. I didn't know what Mama had done until I woke up," Kim continued.

"What about Tracy?" Hard to imagine her standing by while everything unfolded.

"Tracy doesn't know. She thinks Delfina was talking about Mama."

Again, she looked down at Steve. "Mama said the whole thing was really Dad's fault, and that I shouldn't suffer for his mistakes. I wanted to say something, but she said not to. That a smart lawyer would figure out a way to keep her from being in prison too long."

I wondered if Patty also feared Kim wasn't strong enough to handle a trial and imprisonment. Listening to Kim's soft, detached voice, I was worried myself. Not enough to let an innocent woman sit in jail, though.

"I've ruined everything," Kim said. "Daddy's dead. Steve's dead. Mama's in jail."

"You could still fix things," I said. "Tell the police the truth. Explain how it was an accident." Surely the same smart lawyer Patty planned to hire could help Kim.

"I plan to," she said. "I've written everything down. It'll fix everything."

The late morning sun was shining through the transom window, casting shafts of light over Kim and the stairs. It bounced off the object in her hands, leaving tiny rainbows on the wall.

Not an object. A piece of glass. Kim was holding a large shard from the broken wedding photo in her hand.

A sickening realization washed over me. What she meant by fixing everything. The makeup the hair, the lambswool lounge pants, they hadn't been for Steve. They were staging for when they found her.

I needed to distract her. Keep her talking until the EMTs arrived. I strained to hear the sirens. Surely, they were close. When did she call?

"You don't have to do anything drastic," I said. As I talked, I inched my way up the stairs. "I'll go with you to the police. We can tell the police how you were upset and didn't mean to hurt your father. They'll understand."

And then arrest her on the spot, but I left that part out. I'd recite nursery rhymes if they would keep her from putting the glass to her wrist.

"Maybe before, but not now that Steve's dead," Kim said.

"But he's not dead. He's breathing. Look for yourself." I pointed through the railing. If I could get her to look away, I might be able to knock the glass from her hands.

Kim's eyes widened. "Steve's alive?"

"Felt his pulse myself, isn't that right, Steve?" I said, adding silently, *"If you're playing possum, now would be a good time to talk."*

Silence. Not even a groan. Dammit. Whatever doubt I'd started sowing vanished, replaced on Kim's face by a resolved expression. When she spoke, her voice was composed and steady. "This is the only way to fix things. I was going to take pills, but there's not enough time now. Will you tell my mom I'm sorry?"

"I'm not letting you do this," I said.

Her serene smile made my blood go cold. "You don't have a choice."

Hell yeah, I had a choice. As she turned to go upstairs, I hurled myself at her. Like a linebacker taking down a quarterback, I wrapped my arms around her waist and dragged her to the ground. The edge of the stair dug into my back as we landed in a pile. "Let me go," she yelled. Her legs bicycle-kicked in the air as she struggled to break free.

I held fast. The ambulance was coming. The faint sound of sirens could be heard in the distance. If I could keep her from breaking free for another few minutes.

Suddenly, her body stilled. She'd given up. I closed my eyes and let out a sigh of relief. Thank God. It wasn't until her body jerked in my arms that I realized she still held the shard of glass, and her arms were free.

No.

15

———

DAN BARTLETT, Rob, and I sat on the Cho's front step watching as the EMTs loaded Kim, then Steve into the ambulance. Turned out the bastard faking. No sooner did the EMTs pull up, then his eyes opened.

"I should have realized when she stopped struggling," I said. "She gave up too easily." The idea Kim would cut her wrists while I was holding her never crossed my mind. I wanted to kick myself.

"It was a chaotic moment," Bartlett said. "You did the best you could. Be proud of the fact that you had enough presence of mind to tie off her wrists. She'd have lost more blood if you hadn't."

As soon as I'd realized what Kim had done, I ran to her bedroom and grabbed the first thing I could find for a makeshift bandage. That turned out to be a pair of Steve's Italian silk ties. A pretty expensive tourniquet, but then again, the guy'd been willing to let his wife kill herself. I'd just finished tying the second knot when the EMTs arrived. Bartlett followed, while Rob, who heard the address on his scanner app, arrived just after him.

"Dan's right. She probably owes you her life," Rob said.

"I'm not sure Kim appreciates it."

"Maybe not right now, but she will." Bartlett wrapped his arm around my shoulders and pulled me close. Pepperminty warmth washed over me.

Rob, meanwhile, was tutting softly while he cleaned my hands with a wet towel that he'd gotten courtesy of Sean, his EMT. If the situation weren't so horrible, I would feel quite special. "Your coat cuffs are ruined, luv. I'll order you a new one this afternoon. A nice blue wool one."

So long as it wasn't black.

"Delfina confirmed your theory, by the way," Bartlett said. "She didn't see the shooting, but she saw Kim drive away. She went to the wake hoping she could convince Kim to turn herself in. If Kim didn't, she was going to the police herself."

"With all those Cartwrights around, I wouldn't blame her if she thought she was outnumbered that night. Thank goodness she's going to be all right, too. Does all this mean Patty is off the hook?"

"She still faces a few charges for obstructing justice, but mostly, yeah. I owe you and your instincts an apology, Ms. McIntyre. What made you think she was lying to protect Kim?"

"Believe it or not, those turkeys we saw this morning. Talking about mad mother birds made me remember what Patty said at the funeral. Then when Bethany said that Kim knew about the meeting in the park, I knew for certain. Mothers will always protect their children. No matter what."

"Well, next time you have a hunch, I'll listen." He pulled me a little closer and kissed my temple.

In front of his men, too. Did that mean we were a 'we' now? When did that happen? Did I want it to happen?

I stole a look at Bartlett's–Dan's—profile. Yeah, he was worth the risk.

Crap. What was I going to tell Tim?

I'd figure out the answer to that question later. After a hot bath and a long nap. I knew one thing though.

"My hunch days are over. From now on, you're on your own."

"Sure, and I'm going back to wearing gold lamé hats," Rob replied.

I didn't know whose smirk I wanted to wipe off more. They were both annoying. "I'm serious," I said. "I am done playing amateur detective."

For real.

Probably.

Most likely.

I mean, how many more murders could Woodbridge have?

AUTHOR'S NOTE

If you read *Backyards Have Bodies*, you may have noticed that the opening scene from this book differs from how that book ended. Originally, Backyards ended with Sadie receiving an anonymous text that referenced her childhood nickname.

Months after I wrote that scene, I realized I'd written myself into a corner, and that subplot hat detracted from the series' original premise of fun, suburban-set cozy mysteries.

So, I removed the cliffhanger. The prologue you read is how the new version of Backyards ends.

Someday I'll return to Sadie's past and finish her story properly.

Thank you for understanding.

ACKNOWLEDGMENTS

Writing a new Sadie mystery was like slipping on a neglected sweater found in the back of my closet. Sadie's world is so warm and cozy, that I wondered why I hadn't visited earlier.

The answer, of course, is that I was busy working on other projects. I want to give a huge thank you to the readers who emailed me asking when I planned to revisit Woodbridge. I appreciate your patience while I wrote historical fiction, and I hope you found the novella worth the wait. This project wouldn't exist without you.

While I'm expressing gratitude, there are a few other people who deserve a big shout-out:

Thank you, too, to Meena Jain, librarian at the Ashland Public Library for inviting me to the annual Cozy Author Mini Fest. Your invitation was the push I needed to write First Dates.

Thank you to the incomparable Selena Blake of Ecila Media for creating yet another spectacular cover.

Thank you to Donna Alward and Nina Borromeo for their editing and content suggestions. You made this novella better.

Thank you to my writing comrades who are there when I need handholding and brainstorming. You are all rock stars.

Thank you to my son who helped inspire Tim McIntyre. This isn't the first time I've harvested parts of his life for a novel, and I'm sure it won't be the last. Thanks for being such a good sport, Tattoo.

And finally, the biggest thank you to my husband, Peter, who has been on the writing roller coaster with me from the beginning and is my biggest supporter.

ABOUT THE AUTHOR

Barbara Wallace has been an international bestselling author of romance and mystery novels since 2009. Her work has won numerous awards and has been translated into over a dozen languages.

She is also the co-host of Step into the Story, a videocast for lovers of quality historical fiction. The show features book chats, interviews, and writing tips.

When not writing or talking books, Barb can be found herding her three cats, cooing over her grandson, or obsessing over the wildlife in her backyard. She currently lives in New England with her husband and their three incredibly spoiled cats.

Readers are encouraged to sign up for The Barbara Wallace Bulletin. Each week Barb shares essays, reviews, and updates on her current projects. You can sign up through her website at https://www.barbaratannerwallace.com